SPARK THE IMAGINATION

THE SOUTH EAST

YoungWriters

First published in Great Britain in 2008 by
Young Writers, Remus House, Coltsfoot Drive,
Peterborough, PE2 9JX
Tel (01733) 890066 Fax (01733) 313524
All Rights Reserved
Book Design by Tim Christian

Disclaimer
Young Writers has maintained every effort
to publish stories that will not cause offence.
Any stories, events or activities relating to individuals
should be read as fictional pieces and not construed
as real-life character portrayal.

FOREWORD

Young Writers was established in 1990 with the aim of encouraging and nurturing writing skills in young people and giving them the opportunity to see their work in print. By helping them to become more confident and expand their creative skills, we hope our young writers will be encouraged to keep writing as they grow.

Secondary school pupils nationwide have been exercising their minds to create their very own short stories, using no more than fifty words, to be included here in our latest competition *Spark The Imagination.*

The entries we received showed an impressive level of technical skill and imagination, an absorbing look into the eager minds of our future authors.

CONTENTS

THE MINI SAGAS

REFUGEE

Travelling hurts. Everything pain, agony, more and more hurt. Eating nothing. Not even crumbs, garbage, more and more nothing. The world turns smoothly but my feet just plod. The ragged clothes I wear, drag on my bloodstained, sweating body. My tongue's dry, my skin torn; all I feel is pain.

Molly Marshall (12)
BALLARD SCHOOL, NEW MILTON

A RIPPLE IN THE WATER

Frozen snow, cold upon her delicate feet. A soft, slow, falling snowflake gliding down to reach her lips. Never will she know the fear I have feared. Never will she cry for it. A sudden grab, one quick shove, a single shot. A ripple in the water.

Alice Harwood (12)
BALLARD SCHOOL, NEW MILTON

FIREWORKS

Bang! Fire falling from the sky, crashing down to Earth
as cinders. People whooping, clapping, gasping at the
show of colours above. Remembering a man. *Bang!*
Bang! Remembering the Gunpowder Plot. Reflections
in widened eyes, mouths gaping. *Bang!*
A wheel of light. Sparks, flames, screams of joy.
Nights to remember.

Ella Churchill (12)
BALLARD SCHOOL, NEW MILTON

LET THE GALAXY BURN!

Captain Uriel hacked away a limb of an advancing beast. 'Purge them brothers!'
As many were slain, Uriel could taste his victory.
But the attackers launched another volley of troops.
His men were few and far between – wherever the defence was weakest, he would be there for all to see.

Jack Lande [12]
BALLARD SCHOOL, NEW MILTON

4

INDIGO'S SWIM

Indigo was bored. She felt like a swim. She ran down to the beach with her towel and breathed a sigh of relief because she wasn't doing homework. Her dad was nagging on about her English assignment, due in the next day. She dived into the waves, there's a tail!

Samantha Evans (11)
BALLARD SCHOOL, NEW MILTON

THE LONELY NIGHT

Midnight, he was levitating on air. There was a crack, the Earth fractured. A thousand shrieks. Silence. He knew it was Death calling, searing him. That's why he was on an airship, sailing the nights away. Death had found him, the freezing fog rolled in, engulfing him.

Thomas Simpson (12)
BALLARD SCHOOL, NEW MILTON

A NEW START

Kevin walked into the classroom. His clothes were tidy,
for once. He must have taken this new start seriously.
Everyone looked, their eyes glistened.
'You look smart Kevin, now let's smarten up your
English. Do you think you'll fail your test?' said
his teacher.
'Me, fail English. That's umpossible!'

Leila Foale-Groves [11]
BALLARD SCHOOL, NEW MILTON

EXPERIMENT GONE WRONG

I was sitting in chemistry, bored as usual, with chemicals in front of me. The teacher had been explaining for most of the lesson, so wouldn't it be okay to mix up a couple of acids and chemicals? I started to mix different and unusual acids. Nobody noticed ... bad idea!

Charlotte King (12)
BALLARD SCHOOL, NEW MILTON

THIEF

I'm looking through the bushes, carefully watching a
thief. He's just demolished the window, he's snatched
the bags of cash. No! He's spotted me. He's calling for
help. He has a Howitzer. There's a woman walking in
the driveway. The thief's hidden behind the wall.
He's shot her. Police! Police!

Callum Johnstone (12)
BALLARD SCHOOL, NEW MILTON

LOST?

It's there, right in front of me. Mum, Dad and the warmth of a loving home; but it's not real, none of it. I'm lying on the battlefield and everything's lost. I can still feel my heart beating, or maybe it's just my mind mocking me through my despair.

Jasmine Joy Stickley (12)
BALLARD SCHOOL, NEW MILTON

ALLEYWAY CRIME

The flash of a knife blade. Then the echoing bang of a shotgun. A piercing pain zigzags up my body. I drop to the floor, clutching my chest, rocking back and forth. Then the sound of sirens. My so-called friends yell and scatter and I am left, alone.

Jessica Simpkin (12)
BALLARD SCHOOL, NEW MILTON

HAUNTED MANSION

I hear the floorboards creak. I feel the sudden breeze.
Shivers are sent down my spine. The house is
whispering. I run, I run. Round and round to a bare
statue. I feel the words 'you're trapped', I drop
with fear. My mind is blank, I can't get up!

Dom Phillips (11)
BALLARD SCHOOL, NEW MILTON

A STRANGE PLANET

There is a place where no one has been before.
A planet in the distance. A man called Ploverknot, tried
to go up there and explore and discover this planet.
He got in his rocket and flew at 1000mph and got
there in 24 hours and was never seen again.

David Garcia (12)
BALLARD SCHOOL, NEW MILTON

13

WHAT IS IT?

I could hear it now. The *thunk, thunk, thunk* of its footsteps. Was I going crazy? No. The others couldn't hear it, of course not. The steps were louder now, behind me. I tried to tell myself there was nothing there. But then I turned around and saw …

Anja White (13)
BISHOP BELL SCHOOL, EASTBOURNE

LOOKING BACK

It was the day. 19th November 2001. It was quiet, no
one around. The clouds up above, slowly passing by,
like nothing had happened. Everything felt normal,
except that missing feeling inside my tummy. It was as
if I had butterflies, with a guilty feeling.
The day my dad died.

Taylor Greenwood [13]
BROOKFIELD COMMUNITY SCHOOL, SOUTHAMPTON

THE BROWN STRING BRACELET

Red beads fell from a brown string bracelet. Two or three would get stuck in the folds of the floor. The others would glide along their runway until a lady reunited them with their siblings. Relieving them of all their worries, she threaded them back on the brown string bracelet.

Laurel Mae Arnell-Cullen (14)
BROOKFIELD COMMUNITY SCHOOL, SOUTHAMPTON

DIZZY

My face felt like it was pinned back, as I spun round and round, getting dizzier and dizzier. I almost blacked out. As I went up and down, I started to get funny feelings in my stomach. Whizzing around, like it's never going to end … my adventure on the waltzers.

Lucy Welch (13)
BROOKFIELD COMMUNITY SCHOOL, SOUTHAMPTON

17

IT ENDS TONIGHT

Sitting on the ground, my heart broken. Drowning out my cries for help; no one listens anyway. My reflection in the blade; not the person I once knew. No one here; no one to help. Blade against my skin, stab it into my chest. Moments to live. It ends tonight …

Tanya Dashwood (14)
BROOKFIELD COMMUNITY SCHOOL, SOUTHAMPTON

THE PARK

I was walking through the park when it happened. It was a noise so distinct and loud, everyone stood still. Then they were running, running to the point where the noise had come from. Men, women and children, all running to the same place. The ice cream man had arrived!

James Marum (14)
BROOKFIELD COMMUNITY SCHOOL, SOUTHAMPTON

WOODCHUCKS

A woodchuck cannot chuck wood. Although its name is a woodchuck, it cannot chuck wood. No it really can't! A beaver, on the other hand, may be able to throw wood, although it is lacking a thumb!

William Howard (14)
BROOKFIELD COMMUNITY SCHOOL, SOUTHAMPTON

CALL OF DUTY

I was running, bullets flying past my body. The fear was pounding as I ran for my life and then I got hit. Everything went blood-red. I collapsed amongst the chaos. I made my last stand, firing everywhere. Then I fired again. I dropped the controller and left.

Thomas Bailey (14)
BROOKFIELD COMMUNITY SCHOOL, SOUTHAMPTON

MY MINI ADVENTURE

It was a windy day. I lay on the hard ground screaming as I was in pain. My arm wouldn't move, it was broken. I lay in agony, my friends surrounded me. I felt dizzy as I felt a bump on my head. I had fallen from a tree.

Zoe Martin [14]
BROOKFIELD COMMUNITY SCHOOL, SOUTHAMPTON

WHO WILL WIN?

A huge division began up above. What would be defeated? Good or bad? Angels or devils? Heaven or Hell? Which side would come out on top? A battle, the final solution. Which would prove worthy, good or bad? After a close battle the angels beat the devils. Hell was destroyed.

Rachel Millican (13)
BROOKFIELD COMMUNITY SCHOOL, SOUTHAMPTON

ZOOMING CAR

I was unconscious. I stepped out onto the pavement
to find a car zooming straight towards me. I screamed.
The car swerved and rammed into my legs. It felt like a
giant had crushed me all in one. A man rushed out the
car and asked if I was OK!

Felicity Raddon (13)
BROOKFIELD COMMUNITY SCHOOL, SOUTHAMPTON

MY TEA

I was eating my tea. My family sat down with me to
eat their tea. My mum poured me a drink. I drank my
drink, it was blackcurrant. I was enjoying my tea.
I had chicken and chips, in gravy. I finished my tea.
I had enjoyed my tea.

Shane Hatch (13)
BROOKFIELD COMMUNITY SCHOOL, SOUTHAMPTON

ON THE FRONT LINE

I was in the trench with my rifle in hand. I popped my head up as quickly as I could. No one was there. I took a second glance and *bang!* That one second. *Bang!* That one shot, that one movement was it. Nothing more, nothing less. My life ended.

Sam Davy (14)
BROOKFIELD COMMUNITY SCHOOL, SOUTHAMPTON

THE CATASTROPHE

It came crashing down from the sky like a fireball from the heavens. Bits of it flying out everywhere. The main part of the spaceship barely intact. Then the biggest explosion ever as it crashed into the ground. 'Nooo!' The plug from the TV had come out!

Matthew Copland (14)
BROOKFIELD COMMUNITY SCHOOL, SOUTHAMPTON

LONELY HEARTS

Female – though questioned, seeking romance to last a lifetime. Unfortunately bum seems to resemble the continent of Africa – yearning for best friends, undying good looks, clawing onto her last slithers of dignity and her idea of a Saturday night is watching Orlando Bloom, whilst soup boils over in its can.

Jennifer Carson-Paul [14]
BROOKFIELD COMMUNITY SCHOOL, SOUTHAMPTON

FEAR OF HEIGHTS

My knees trembling, I peer down at the ground
beneath me. A gust of wind brushes my cheek, tiny
hairs stand up on my arms. I jump! Falling rapidly.
I scream for help. *Bang!*
'What are you doing by this rusty bench? Break time's
over, now back to lessons please!'

Charlotte Simmons (14)
BROOKFIELD COMMUNITY SCHOOL, SOUTHAMPTON

29

THE ADVENTURE

All I could see was foliage. So many different plants hitting me in so many different places. It was hot, unbearable, but I was alone. There was no one, no hope – or was there? I heard voices in the distance and beeping. It was a checkout. Phew! I'm in Garsons.

Dom Court (14)
BROOKFIELD COMMUNITY SCHOOL, SOUTHAMPTON

NIGHTMARE CAVE

I was being chased. I ran and I ran through the dark cave, bats taunting me with their shadows. Then turning a corner, I fell. A light! I desperately scrambled to my feet. Running and running, I was suddenly stopped in my tracks by a piercing sound.
My alarm clock!

Emily Gaebler (14)
BROOKFIELD COMMUNITY SCHOOL, SOUTHAMPTON

31

SUMMER'S BREEZE

Lying in the sun, this is the life. Children laughing, sun shining, waves swaying to and fro. The pearly white sand between my toes. The gentle breeze swifting it into a tornado of summer. My life a distant memory, as I calmly drift away with that warm, gentle summer's breeze.

Donna Edwards (14)
BROOKFIELD COMMUNITY SCHOOL, SOUTHAMPTON

MY JOURNEY

I walked through the square, grey machine hoping
it would remain silent. Continuing to collect my bag,
I swung it over my shoulder and carried on to join
the next queue. I'd been standing for hours, and felt
relieved to sit on the plane and fly off to another land.

Georgia Foy (13)
BROOKFIELD COMMUNITY SCHOOL, SOUTHAMPTON

EXPLORER

Click! Lights had gone. I was alone against the world. I climbed mountains, a small glow of light in the distance. I crawled through tunnels and forests. Suddenly I was surrounded. An ambush! One-eyed bears, ferocious to behold! I couldn't escape.
Light appeared.
'Stop playing. Bedtime!' said Mum.

Zoe Peterkin (14)
BROOKFIELD COMMUNITY SCHOOL, SOUTHAMPTON

PEN AND PAPER

I was staring at the paper, looking for a first line. Pen
made contact. Words formed. In-between lines, black
ink rolled across the page. Things were starting to look
good, a story forming. With things looking good,
I brought this to an end and put down this black pen.

Karl Tate (14)
BROOKFIELD COMMUNITY SCHOOL, SOUTHAMPTON

PLANE CRASH

The plane took off, soaring through the air. Turning, gliding, *crash!* There was crying, wailing. The amazing greatest plane, gone! Smashed into a million pieces. I stood up, unhurt, looking around through my water-filled eyes. Gone. My whole world torn apart.
I picked up my toy plane and left.

James Caldwell (14)
BROOKFIELD COMMUNITY SCHOOL, SOUTHAMPTON

QUICKSAND

I clambered through dense jungle, until I found the submerged cave; shovelling, pushing and scraping to pry inside. Once inside, shining my torch to see through the dark abyss. Then suddenly I was drowning, sinking deeper and deeper until I thought I felt the clutches of Hell, squeezing me blue …

Hannah Vincent (14)
BROOKFIELD COMMUNITY SCHOOL, SOUTHAMPTON

TOUCHING THE CLOUDS

I climbed and climbed, wind in my hair. Touching the clouds. There was one way out but I'm scared of heights. I couldn't look down. Just the thought made me scared.
Then out of nowhere, Daddy helped me down and said, 'Don't you want to go on the slide now?'

Jordan Waller (14)
BROOKFIELD COMMUNITY SCHOOL, SOUTHAMPTON

YOUNG LOVE

I waited, he waited, we waited for each other. Down the bumpy lane, hand in hand we strolled. Above us, the sky as blue as could be. Beneath us, the lush, green grass. No one around, just me and him. Time to say goodbye. Closer we came, gently we kissed.

Kirsty Pottinger (14)
BROOKFIELD COMMUNITY SCHOOL, SOUTHAMPTON

39

MY SPACESHIP

3 … 2 … 1 … blast-off! Finally … the dream of my life.
I soar past planets and stars. Who knows who or what
I'll meet. Maybe a friendly alien who will show what
Mars bars are really made of. Then …
'Tea's ready, get out of your box for today!'
'Ohhh!'

Charlotte Merrikin (13)
BROOKFIELD COMMUNITY SCHOOL, SOUTHAMPTON

THE BEST DAY EVER

I felt like Cinderella. My fairy-tale dress and my Prince
Charming on my arm. I floated down the aisle, the
smile couldn't be wiped off my face for anything.
Best day ever. 'I do,' I exclaimed.
'Okay, my turn to be the bride,' begged Kate.
'Take turns,' said Mum.

Alexandra Ord (14)
BROOKFIELD COMMUNITY SCHOOL, SOUTHAMPTON

41

THE SPRINT TO NOWHERE

Climbing in his wheel, shaking off unwanted dust. Let's
go, run, run, run. Stop for a moment, take a breath.
Let's go, run, run, run. One more rest, quickly wiping
his brow. Let's go, run, run, run. Been going
for a while. Finally my hamster collapses,
realising he's going nowhere.

Rachel Farnan (14)
BROOKFIELD COMMUNITY SCHOOL, SOUTHAMPTON

CAR CRASH

A lazy Sunday morning. Driving down the motorway.
Windows open, it's too hot in the car. Talking to
parents, nothing else to do. Piece of wreckage in the
road. Accidentally tip the wheel. Car spins. Car flips.
Car bursts into flames. Just like me.
My entire world up in flames.

Christopher Giles [13]
BROOKFIELD COMMUNITY SCHOOL, SOUTHAMPTON

43

PERIOD THREE

The pain, it grows as I sit here. This torture, it will never stop. Please make it stop. I can't take it anymore. But the torture goes on and on. I feel like screaming. The pain is too much. Then the bell goes and period three maths is over.

Ed Russell (14)
BROOKFIELD COMMUNITY SCHOOL, SOUTHAMPTON

LUCKY ME?

Eating lunch, I heard screeching from above. Seagulls!
Flying rats! Swoop, swoop. People screamed and
scattered from their groups of friends. Poop, poop, on
the other poor suckers. Everyone screaming around
me, running for shelter. Something white: Bird? Insect?
Catch of light? *Ew!* Just my luck! I got pooped on!

Laura Parry (14)
BROOKFIELD COMMUNITY SCHOOL, SOUTHAMPTON

MARXUS TERINIUS

A soldier stumbled from the fire, sword clutched in one hand. He stood taller than a tree and had the look of a warrior shining in his eyes. His helmet in his hand, he uttered ten words. 'Hey guys do you mind if I take a break?'
'Cut!'
'Toilet, quickly!'

Ben Sherwood (14)
BROOKFIELD COMMUNITY SCHOOL, SOUTHAMPTON

DROP THE GUN

'Drop the gun!'
Fear rushed through me. What was happening?
'I'm not letting her go!'
What was I hearing?
'Drop the weapon!'
Bang! Child death.
'Somebody chase him!'
All I could see was black. I heard my mother.
'Quick Josie, wake up! CSI is on.'

Josie Chapman-Ward (14)
BROOKFIELD COMMUNITY SCHOOL, SOUTHAMPTON

47

ON THE SWING

I was flying high. Feet pointing towards the sky, arms soaring. I was almost touching the clouds, could feel the wind in my hair. My heart was going to burst, I was so happy. But then a voice sliced through my ecstasy. 'Off the swings now darling! We're going home.'

Kayley Barnes (13)
BROOKFIELD COMMUNITY SCHOOL, SOUTHAMPTON

IT'S ALL YOUR FAULT

Trapped in the room, pens scurrying across the paper. Heavy breathing in and out. But why? Concealed from the outside world like an innocent rabbit caged in its hutch. Tugging at my hair, pulling vigorously at my book; I scream, 'It's all your fault … you and your mini sagas.' Typical!

Johanna Wagstaffe (13)
BROOKFIELD COMMUNITY SCHOOL, SOUTHAMPTON

THE LOVE OF MY LIFE

My heart thumped in my chest. He was the perfect guy; cute, considerate and a thirst for blood. The perfect guy, in my eyes anyway. He loved to snuggle my neck, so I thought. I found it sweet until he went a bit too far. Now the night's my playground.

Karelia Rice (13)
BROOKFIELD COMMUNITY SCHOOL, SOUTHAMPTON

POO

'Mummy, what's poo?'
Oh God, I thought, *how do I explain? Should I ring Dad? No, just improvise.* I could feel sweat running down my spine. 'Well dear … and that's poo!'
'Oh, OK Mummy, so what is Tigger?'

Soozii Francis (13)
BROOKFIELD COMMUNITY SCHOOL, SOUTHAMPTON

WHAT AM I?

It's a hard life, stuck in a small claustrophobic place,
barely allowed out unless words are written on the
page. Why could I not have a better life like the friends
I live with? I shrink every time I am used! What am I?
A pencil! (Obvious or what?)

Carla Bannister (13)
BROOKFIELD COMMUNITY SCHOOL, SOUTHAMPTON

THE MASSACRE

Slice! Slice! Slice! I cut them. I catch them.
I hunt them. From their plastic habitat, they squeal,
they cry, they bleed. As I cut and gut them, I shove
them in the blazing pan. I smell their burning flesh.
'Those peppers look nice Kian!'

Kian Behdoost (13)
BROOKFIELD COMMUNITY SCHOOL, SOUTHAMPTON

ONE TOO MANY

The sweat dripped from my face as I fiddled with my pen. I was running out of time but I was thinking hard. I was about to give up as it came to me. I've never worked so hard in my life. But it was finished. Bummer – fifty-one words!

Steffan Davies (13)
BROOKFIELD COMMUNITY SCHOOL, SOUTHAMPTON

SNOWBOARD AND MY MUM

I balanced on my board, concentrating. White snow
glistened all around. I saw Mum in the distance.
She was waving crazily, thinking I couldn't see her.
Approaching her, I turned quickly and massive
amounts of snow flew up. Looking round there was
no Mum, only a huge pile of snow!

George Stokes (13)
BROOKFIELD COMMUNITY SCHOOL, SOUTHAMPTON

HAMLET (MODERN VERSION)

'You will lose Lord Hamlet,' said Horatio.
'I do not think so, I have a nuclear device in hand!'
Laertes walks in, AK47 ready. He loads, shoots, then
bang! A mushroom cloud fills the sky.
'Shame,' said Gertrude, whipping out her
fully-charged discombobulator gun. She disintegrates
King Claudius.

James Thomas (13)
BROOKFIELD COMMUNITY SCHOOL, SOUTHAMPTON

GAME OVER

Four enemies. I pulled out an assault rifle and screwed
on a silencer. I was breathing heavily now. They saw
me. I threw a smoke grenade and sprinted past and
suddenly stopped. Where was the stupid X button?
I yelled, as I threw the PlayStation controller
across the room.

Jack Taylor [13]
BROOKFIELD COMMUNITY SCHOOL, SOUTHAMPTON

57

PAIN

The sharp, unforgettable pain shot through my body,
piercing, tearing. It felt like every muscle in my body
was tense, waiting for the horror, the pain that would
once again torture me with its stabbing …
Why did I buy these shoes? I guess seventy pounds
was too good an offer …

Millie Aldridge (13)
BROOKFIELD COMMUNITY SCHOOL, SOUTHAMPTON

THE VOYAGE

Screens flicker. Nothing but darkness,
like a never-ending black hole. There is a sudden
silence. I hear my heart beat like a cheetah ready to
pounce. Am I alone? Is anyone there? Could this be
the end of not only you but me as well?
There's nothing but darkness.

Megan Dennis (12)
BROOKFIELD COMMUNITY SCHOOL, SOUTHAMPTON

59

ALONE

As I sat downstairs, my brother went up. He heard a
noise, 'Anyone there?' No reply. He came down.
Slash. Someone had stabbed him.
My mum got home. *Bang! Bang!* On the floor she fell.
Now I was alone with who or what.
'Help me! Somebody help me!'

Callum Liddle (12)
BROOKFIELD COMMUNITY SCHOOL, SOUTHAMPTON

THE SNIPER SLEEPS

The sniper sits, still. As the sweat trickles down his face, he waits silently for the enemy. He hears a noise. Tensing all the muscles in his body, he concentrates into the gun's sight. Zooming closer and closing – *bang!* As the bullet travels, he knows it is too late.

Ollie Nail (12)
BROOKFIELD COMMUNITY SCHOOL, SOUTHAMPTON

A HARD LIFE

Stop kicking me bully. Why are you doing this to me?
It's not good, stop cheering, put me down. There's
one of me and twenty-two of them. I'm going up.
Argh! I'm coming down again, it's horrible.
I hate this job, it's hard being a football.

Jack Gentles (12)
BROOKFIELD COMMUNITY SCHOOL, SOUTHAMPTON

THE SCORPION

I was being my usual self. Wearing black, preparing
to stab at the right time. The time ticked by. I waited.
My victim bent down. The time was right. I struck with
force. As I watched it suffer and fall to the ground,
I realised it's good being a scorpion.

Simon Roland (12)
BROOKFIELD COMMUNITY SCHOOL, SOUTHAMPTON

SNAILS ARE VERY EVIL

They were coming. I knew this day would come. They would destroy my race. We got into battle positions. There were more of us than them. We could win … We lost. I was the last man standing. The snails came to eat me. I hate being a cabbage!

Jasmine Brown (11)
BROOKFIELD COMMUNITY SCHOOL, SOUTHAMPTON

RUGBY

Walking towards the field of fresh green grass,
I saw the sun rising. Teams were gathered in groups.
We were called in, then got into our positions. The ref
placed the ball down, then blew his mighty whistle.
We battled and fought and all of a sudden,
I blacked out …

Jay Patel (12)
BROOKFIELD COMMUNITY SCHOOL, SOUTHAMPTON

PASSION

Passion! Swords clashing, lightning blinds my
electrified eyes. The fight races against my pounding
heart, will I win? Will we be finished? Bravely battling
on, our bloodthirsty war continues.
A glimpse of a witness loses my nerve. Suddenly,
a thunderous bang shocks our scene. The bell.
Drama class ends.

Jennifer White (14)
BROOKFIELD COMMUNITY SCHOOL, SOUTHAMPTON

SOARIN'

Heart hammering through my chest, legs trembling
with fear. Will this nightmare ever end? Thoughts
running through my mind. Shall I jump?
My mind's made up.
Flying through the atmosphere, held up by howling
wind. My body hits the wood. I soar through the air,
gripping tightly to the swing.

Lauren Heno (14)
BROOKFIELD COMMUNITY SCHOOL, SOUTHAMPTON

CAN YOU FEEL THE PRESSURE?

It screamed to be shook. Gas building up, swelling. Thick seething black liquid rose up. Pressure, compulsion, strain. Was it going to blow? Adrenalin squeezed through my pulsating veins. Five, four, three, two, one ... it erupted. Syrupy, fizzing Coke splattered my face and evaporated off, leaving a layer of sugar.

Shannon Hoey (15)
BROOKFIELD COMMUNITY SCHOOL, SOUTHAMPTON

FALLING

I was plummeting towards the ground. My face, white as snow. There was nothing I could do. My entire life flashed before my eyes. *Why did I do it? Why?* These thoughts were going round my head. It ended as suddenly as it started. I disembarked the roller coaster.

Cameron Pye (14)
BROOKFIELD COMMUNITY SCHOOL, SOUTHAMPTON

THE DARKNESS

Waking up in a burning sweat, my eyes, blinded by the
blackest silence. Can I survive this? My head spins.
Shuddering, I creep my way to the door, clutching
onto anything I can. My heart races, I still can't see.
A slash of light … the power cut is finally over.

Lauren Pontin (14)
BROOKFIELD COMMUNITY SCHOOL, SOUTHAMPTON

WHAT GOES UP ...

Wandering through a world of blurred beasts, his head
seemed to rotate upon its connection to his being.
Creatures rushed past, ape-like in posture, all different
shapes and sizes, clutching their nostrils. Suddenly
dragged to the ground by an invisible ghoul.
He whispered to himself, 'No more drugs man!'

Samuel Slamaker (13)
BROOKFIELD COMMUNITY SCHOOL, SOUTHAMPTON

71

THE DARKNESS

Darkness everywhere. I'm scared. How did I get here?
What happened? I see monsters everywhere. A bear.
What to do! I hear footsteps, something to save me or
get me? No it's here! I duck in desperation.
The door creaks open and the being says,
'My turn to hide!'

Adrian Cross (14)
BROOKFIELD COMMUNITY SCHOOL, SOUTHAMPTON

THE DREADED THING

Oh no, it's at my feet, the dreaded thing. It attracts all of them. Their broad, muscular bodies charge. I'm stranded, all alone. My comrades have abandoned me. Howling like wolves. As if to taunt me in their freedom. I kick that thing frantically. *Goal!*

Rob Clinch (14)
BROOKFIELD COMMUNITY SCHOOL, SOUTHAMPTON

NUNS AND BUNS

The nuns ran out of the bank doors, arms loaded with cash, to buy buns. They ran straight into the busy street. They accidentally hit a policeman, who had just received word of a group of nuns on the run! They were arrested for having an abundance of money!

Jon Butt (14)
CARISBROOKE HIGH SCHOOL, NEWPORT

HOW DO YOU REALLY KNOW?

How do you know you're standing where you are? How do you know you're seeing what you see? How do you know your friends are there? How do you know you awoke this morning? How do you know it's not your imagination? You don't know if it is or not …

Aaron Christopher Dowden (14)
CARISBROOKE HIGH SCHOOL, NEWPORT

RETRIBUTION

Overcast clouds billow ceaselessly. Silent, yet poised
he lies, awaiting the victim. Engulfed by smoke,
coughed from bronchial chimneys. Watching the
hotel. Water cascades down his eyes. Eyes of a
leopard. Remorseless. A door swinging. The chatter of
unconcerned, cheerful voices. Prey. One shot to ease
painful memory. One shot …

Charlie Ferguson (14)
CARISBROOKE HIGH SCHOOL, NEWPORT

THE TOWERS

The deafening noise of an angry jet turbine, whined over the streets of New York. The low-flying aircraft collided with the towers. The impact split the towers. They toppled onto the busy streets below. The death toll was never discovered. The disaster lay a hidden mystery.

Charlie Norman (11)
CHRIST THE KING COLLEGE, NEWPORT

TWO TRAGIC LIVES

Two extraordinary friends met each other in a small barn. The pig was the runt and the spider lived on her own. They had great fun together and helped each other out as friends should … Until the spider laid her eggs and died and the pig became fat, juicy bacon.

Bethany Capon (11)
CHRIST THE KING COLLEGE, NEWPORT

TITANIC TRAGEDY

The unsinkable sank, the innocent died, tears rolled down his cheeks. His lover, gone. Whimpers came from her mouth – Mother's overboard. The cold sea grabbed the vessel down. Glass windows shattered. Then a scream. I pulled my cushion in front of my face. All over, all dead.

Jasmin Spence (11)
CHRIST THE KING COLLEGE, NEWPORT

MOVING HOUSE

Clear out room, empty house and rooms echo. Don't
want to go. Won't go. Shove suitcases in the car.
Slump in the car seat, while saying goodbye to my old
home. Don't want to go. Won't go. Drive along roads.
All new places. See new house. I like it here!

Katherine Wheeler (10)
CHRIST THE KING COLLEGE, NEWPORT

RUN

I heard a faint noise in the distance behind. I looked
and stared in horror. I knew I had to do something or
lives would be lost. Innocent lives, lives of those near
to me. What shall I do? Where shall I go?
I have to save them. Run!

James Shelley (11)
CHRIST THE KING COLLEGE, NEWPORT

WRECKED BEAUTY

Such a disaster: first voyage – also last. That nasty
hard water. That helpful soft water. Scary feelings.
What should they have done? Why didn't they choose
safety? Captain devastated. It was a normal year,
1912, until the worst tragedy plunged Southampton
into sorrow. The result: few survivors,
one wrecked beauty.

Emma Forrest (11)
CHRIST THE KING COLLEGE, NEWPORT

WANTED! DEAD OR ASLEEP

Asleep for one hundred years. Covered in dust,
lying there; dead like. Slowly moulding, like an old
uneaten sandwich that has been left in the corner of a
breadbin. Another one hundred years gone! Mythical
fairies flutter around their heads,
'Will they wake?' they whisper. I doubt it.

Polly Hayden (11)
CHRIST THE KING COLLEGE, NEWPORT

FAIRY TALE TWIST

Glittering chandeliers, moonlit windows, prince strolls
into prom, glancing at the rainbow of girls. Boredom
grows. A pure white girl appears, love at first sight.
Getting late, the girl disappears; a slipper is left.
The slave works hard. Her dream comes true.
The prince finds his true love at last.

Rebecca Herman (11)
CHRIST THE KING COLLEGE, NEWPORT

THE WOOD KILLING

Panting, legs pumping, heart thumping, running, running. Getting darker, must keep going, don't stop. He's chasing me. Gonna kill me. I'm gonna die. Jumping over logs, dodging trees. He's quicker, I'm tired. My life just seemed to get worse. Suddenly, he ran off and didn't return but this hadn't ended.

Harry Stagg (11)
CHRIST THE KING COLLEGE, NEWPORT

GINGER

His eyes are simple Smarties, same with his mouth
and nose. He is sweet in both ways and is made out
of the tastiest ginger. He is friends with a muffin man.
He is a cross between a cookie and a man. Can you
guess who he is? *Munch! Crunch!*

Caroline Hawkins (11)
CHRIST THE KING COLLEGE, NEWPORT

A SMALL WORLD

I once was in a world when I was big, but now I'm in a world of small. The doors were small, but now are normal, the table is massive, but then was perfect. All I needed was a little sip of the thing that makes you small forever.

Paige Guy (10)
CHRIST THE KING COLLEGE, NEWPORT

87

AIME'S POND VS DR MOO
WHO WILL WIN?

Aime's pond stood still with a machine gun in his hands. *Bang!* A huge bullet fled across the room and straight into Dr Moo's stomach. He fell to the ground. Suddenly he got back up and laughed. He said, 'You will never be able to kill me!'

Lucy Blake (11)
CHRIST THE KING COLLEGE, NEWPORT

BANG!

Bang! Bang! Bang! I heard those knocks again. An equal space between them. I asked my friend what it was but he didn't know. A thing. *Bang! Bang! Bang!* There, those bangs. *Bang … bang … smash* - an axe crashed through the door and there he was, the killer, stained blood-red.

Cameron Law (11)
CHRIST THE KING COLLEGE, NEWPORT

THE GREAT

The ship is heading towards danger; the waves
crashing into the boat. People are everywhere, running
to fragile lifeboats. The captain is trying to calm the
children. Another smash! The deck shakes again.
The ship sinks quicker. People are getting thrown
overboard. A last scream for help. Too late!

Daniel Simpkins (11)
CHRIST THE KING COLLEGE, NEWPORT

CINDERELLA'S AUDITIONS

Cinderella was auditioning princes. Her stepsisters were stealing them. First up was Jack (famous for his beanstalk). 'No good!' exclaimed Cinderella. 'Too farmer-like.' Then she tried Prince Charming. As soon as Cinderella saw him, she knew he was right for her. But the prince fell for her sister.

Charlotte Hall (10)
CHRIST THE KING COLLEGE, NEWPORT

DOOMED

The clouds crept in and the wind whistled through the drains. *Knock, knock, knock!* I stared in horror at the outline of the figure less than a few steps away from me. The window smashed, the TV turned off, power cut. Good DVD though!

Nathan Webb (11)
CHRIST THE KING COLLEGE, NEWPORT

JUNGLE MAN

Through the leaves of the jungle, a man was swinging from branch to branch. Among the leaves there were deadly animals waiting to grab him. There were spiders and other treacherous things. As he was swinging from branch to branch, something bit him, he fell to the ground. He'd failed.

Laura Overton (11)
CHRIST THE KING COLLEGE, NEWPORT

93

THE MYSTERY OF AGATHA CHRISTIE

Mrs Christie parked her car on the riverside at midnight. Suddenly, she saw a spark of light. She walked over to the light and she saw an alien creature. It grabbed her and she screamed.
Ten days later she appeared at a hotel with no memories of what had happened.

Joshua Attrill (11)
CHRIST THE KING COLLEGE, NEWPORT

STARS IN HER EYES

With long, flowing blonde hair and stars in her twinkling eyes, she twirled to the music and smiled at the glinting lights. Her dashing clothes were all the rage in fashion magazines. Everyone wanted to be her. The music ended. She put the hairbrush down.

Éloise Radestock (11)
CHRIST THE KING COLLEGE, NEWPORT

ALICE'S NEW ROOM

Falling, falling, slower, slower. Leaves crackle. Alice halts. Door so small, bottle so large, drink. Now comes a smaller life. Key too big, key too high. So eat cake so small to become so tall. So now stuck in that room for all eternity. Waiting to become nothing at all.

Heather Simpson (11)
CHRIST THE KING COLLEGE, NEWPORT

SPY

'Come on, shh, they'll see us!'
'No they won't! Ah-ha! Here we go.'
'Have you got it?'
'Yeah.'
'Give it here then.'
'No. I was told to trust no one.'
'Give over! Now in it goes and we're done.
We've succeeded.'
'Yes!'
'Shh.'
'Yes, yes! I know'
'Shh!'

Katie Durkin (11)
CHRIST THE KING COLLEGE, NEWPORT

SPIRAL OF DEATH

One summer's day some friends were out canoeing.
They were having a brilliant time. Then, suddenly their
peace was destroyed. There was a whirling typhoon.
They were swirling round and round and round. They
were trying their hardest to get out but it didn't work.
They were sucked in.

Edward Lloyd (11)
CHRIST THE KING COLLEGE, NEWPORT

UNTITLED

One day, my sisters received an invitation to a ball, but of course, I did not. Soon the occasion was here and my sisters left. Suddenly I was transformed into something beautiful. There I danced with the perfect man but the time had come for me to leave.

Abigail Rudd (11)
CHRIST THE KING COLLEGE, NEWPORT

GOLDEN CITY BENEATH THE SPARKLING WAVES

Sunk out of sight. Its old walls crumbled. Fish were the only residents, as everybody else had departed. But as it was rediscovered, life began to spring. Gold leaf crept over walls again; silver platters were laden with food. Life was restored to the golden city beneath the sparkling waves.

Elizabeth Parsons (11)
CHRIST THE KING COLLEGE, NEWPORT

THE CHASE

Bang! Another nuclear bomb had just gone off, this one in Rio. They had to get their man. The trail was getting fainter. Their hopes were drifting away, like feathers in the breeze. Then nothing. The ground was a smooth plate of jungle mud. He was gone. They had failed.

Sam Barber (11)
CHRIST THE KING COLLEGE, NEWPORT

101

MOVING HOUSE - WHY?

In my room, thinking hard. What is it going to be like?
What about my friends? If I get bullied and don't fit in?
I haven't seen the house inside.
Will there be rats or mice? Nobody knows.
On the other hand, it could be great.

Dan Mew (11)
CHRIST THE KING COLLEGE, NEWPORT

ESCAPE ROUTE

Blazing rays of light shone down on the glistening sand. I sprawled out, in the hope that a rescuer would arrive. It was a microscopic island, the size of a ten-foot trampoline. I'd been there for days, just living on coconuts from the two palm trees.
Waiting, waiting, waiting …

Bradley Sheath (11)
CHRIST THE KING COLLEGE, NEWPORT

THE CHRONICLES OF NARNIA

Peter, Susan, Edmund, Lucy. They found a place called Narnia. They met Mr Tumnus - killed him at first sight. Befriended the badgers, got the information they needed and ditched them. Who needs badgers? Finally they found the White Witch who turned them into stone. Isn't it so lovely in Narnia!

Jess Brooke [11]
CHRIST THE KING COLLEGE, NEWPORT

WAR WITH BRICKS, WOOD AND HAY

The bad wolf was seen over the horizon, but this time, the three little pigs had their cannons at the ready. A horn blew, war commenced. The pigs fired whatever they had, bricks, wood and hay. Now on the sunny horizon was a big, bad, dead wolf!

Toby Utteridge (11)
CHRIST THE KING COLLEGE, NEWPORT

MOVING HOUSE

Boxes packed and all in the car. Doors and windows
locked. Drive through the countryside for the final time.
Walking through the woods to get to their location.
In bed, hearing eerie noises from outside. Walking
outside. He has a fox following him and …

Rebecca Ashcroft (11)
CHRIST THE KING COLLEGE, NEWPORT

JAMES POND!

The anticipation was vast, as Bond sped along the riverside, making sure that his enemy was no more than three metres ahead. Bond had been chasing Zao (his enemy) for way too long. Bond released his wheel blade, drove up beside Zao but *splash!* Bond had fallen into the river.

Jack McGrath (11)
CHRIST THE KING COLLEGE, NEWPORT

107

METEOR SHOWER

Falling stars. That's what they are. Unspeakable beauty. They light up the sky for a split second. Follow them and you will see them fly past you, burning up in a fiery ball of dust. Here for a second and then they vanish as if nothing has happened.

Grace Oliver (11)
CHRIST THE KING COLLEGE, NEWPORT

SNOW WHITE

A perfect girl moves into a house with seven dwarfs.
I hear they're very hospitable. The evil witch plots a
plan that could cost the young girl her life. Lying in
her coffin, a prince comes along to see. One kiss and
back to life happily ever after.

Jasmine Greenwood (11)
CHRIST THE KING COLLEGE, NEWPORT

RACING HERO ... DEAD

It was the final race. If Japeth could do this, he would become the motorcycle champion of all time.
He would be a star!
Then it happened, he was nearing the final corner, suddenly ... the bike tipped, petrol poured out, a spark caused flames. That day, a life was taken!

Hannah Millgate (10)
CHRIST THE KING COLLEGE, NEWPORT

THE DARK NIGHT

On a dark and gloomy night, a young boy was lying awake in bed. The dim light of the street light outside of his window suddenly went out and the sound of the TV stopped. Silence. He started to tremble with fear. Should he investigate who was behind his door?

Samuel Crofts (13)
FERNHILL SCHOOL & LANGUAGE COLLEGE, FARNBOROUGH

111

EXPLOSION

Crash! Smack! Right in the face. Bleeding like someone screaming. Falling 100 feet into a crater. *Crash! Crack!* Squealing like a fox. Still running through the rough trees swaying like a rag doll. *Boom! Shake!* Finally I'm away. Seriously injured, looking back at the explosion. Watching people die in pain.

Jordan Westrup (13)
FERNHILL SCHOOL & LANGUAGE COLLEGE, FARNBOROUGH

THE FAIRGROUND

The hottest day. Crowds wandering around. Laughter, music and shouting. Suddenly sobbing. A child on his own. 'Help, help!' Panicking as people search for Mum. Scared and frightened of what could happen. Suddenly out of the crowds rushes Mum. Hugs and kisses. Happy again so the party goes on.

Courtney Turner (13)
FERNHILL SCHOOL & LANGUAGE COLLEGE, FARNBOROUGH

STEALTH

The sound of the countdown, makes you have an adrenalin rush straight through your body. In two point eight seconds you reach eighty miles per hour. You climb two hundred and five feet, then suddenly drop down again. Your stomach lurches as your body jerks over the final bump.

Kieran Tuffnell (13)
FERNHILL SCHOOL & LANGUAGE COLLEGE, FARNBOROUGH

PIKES IN THE LAKE

There were pikes in the lake. A woman with long hair came crying by the lake, walking a small dog on a lead. The dog stood in the water and the pike caught it by the leg, pulled it under. The woman let go of the lead, left, still crying.

Aiden Upward (13)
FERNHILL SCHOOL & LANGUAGE COLLEGE, FARNBOROUGH

STEALTH

I sat on the seat. I knew there was no turning back.
I held tight. Three, two, one, Go! I couldn't breathe.
I was held back. I couldn't lean I looked down. I flew
towards the floor. 205 feet in the air. I survived the
highest ride in the UK.

Ashleigh Richardson (13)
FERNHILL SCHOOL & LANGUAGE COLLEGE, FARNBOROUGH

EXPLOSION

Rumble, explosion, ash everywhere. People screaming
and then the lava falling two hundred feet into a
crater. Burning heat, people running and screaming.
Watching people dying. The lava is running down the
hill and it is covering everything in its way.
The village is destroyed.

Nicholas Smith (12)
FERNHILL SCHOOL & LANGUAGE COLLEGE, FARNBOROUGH

TIDAL WAVE

Sitting in the seat gently locked in. I was terrified
I would fall to my death. We climbed up and up, really
slowly. I was scared this was the start of my death.
We reached the top. It was time to go into the deep
water below, to my death!

Ashley Bubb (13)
FERNHILL SCHOOL & LANGUAGE COLLEGE, FARNBOROUGH

MY NEW PUPPY

Ring! I answer.
'Get downstairs now!'
They hang up. I'm terrified. What's happened?
I hear the front door opening. My mum has a towel
in her arms. Stumbling into the living room I stare.
Unwrapping the towel there's a bundle of spotty,
soft fur. My adorable little new puppy.

Amy Cann [13]
FERNHILL SCHOOL & LANGUAGE COLLEGE, FARNBOROUGH

119

THE NOT SO PERFECT MOMENT

He was leaning towards me making a move. It was the
most perfect moment of my life, until I opened my eyes
and looked up and saw a horror! Yuck! It was my dog
waking me up! Licking my face! Now I wish I'd never
got him! Silly, stupid dog!

Abbie Howard (12)
FERNHILL SCHOOL & LANGUAGE COLLEGE, FARNBOROUGH

FORTY-EIGHT HOURS

Can't wait until this weekend – so excited! We have a
fabulous forty-eight hours of full-on partying. Meeting
at the bowling alley, then cheesy pizza with a midnight
makeover and sleepover! Awaking to a waterslide
barbecue, you will never forget with a snoring snooze.
Monday – English *yawn, zzzz* …

Bethany Morris (12)
PATCHAM HIGH SCHOOL, PATCHAM

UNTITLED

Three pigs went to Burger King because they didn't like the cow who was being cooked, because he bullied them when they were growing up. They ate him in a bun with chips and a Coke but the owner ran out of bacon and he wanted a bacon sandwich. Run!

Luke Johnson (13)
PATCHAM HIGH SCHOOL, PATCHAM

SPIRITED AWAY

On the first night there was a knock. I didn't answer,
I was too tired. On the second night there were two
knocks but I was still too tired. On the third night
I answered it. It was my father, but he's dead.
Now I knock on my mother's door.

Sam White (12)
PATCHAM HIGH SCHOOL, PATCHAM

HOLIDAY ADVENTURE

The holiday adventure. Sun shining over the horizon,
birds singing and the fresh water hitting the rocks.
Have a dip in the pool and a relaxing shower.
Evening approaches and the sun goes down to rest.
The moon comes out to brighten up the sky.
The peaceful night sky.

Harry Doogan (12)
PATCHAM HIGH SCHOOL, PATCHAM

UNTITLED

Love is like an ocean which is brighter than the sun. It gleams, so sparkly it's like glitter. It makes your eyes shine and your diamond bling sparkle. Your phone rings at the speed of light. After tomorrow the glitter will turn orange, so bright, like flowers that shine.

Courtney Pankhurst (12)
PATCHAM HIGH SCHOOL, PATCHAM

WHY ME?

Miss told us to do the fifty word story but I knew
I wasn't going to win, so I could not be bothered. But,
I had to count the words. It's annoying me, so I tried to
think of a story but I could not. I dreamt that I had won.

Samuel Keeley (12)
PATCHAM HIGH SCHOOL, PATCHAM

SCHOOL

Children tapping their pens on the desks, waiting for
the bell. The angry teacher shouting about mistakes.
Students asking the time. Chairs scraping on the floor
with fidgeting. 'Can we go yet please?'
I'm hungry and tired. Three minutes till the bell.
Finally it rings!

Rebecca Knight (12)
PATCHAM HIGH SCHOOL, PATCHAM

TERRANCE AND THE DISASTROUS APPLE

A pig called Terrance climbed up a tree to get an apple for his mother. Terrance saw a golden apple. *We'd have enough money to buy apples,* he thought. *Yes, got it!* Terrance fell out of the tree and died. The wolf nicked it. That was the end of Terrance.

Billy Braiden (12)
PATCHAM HIGH SCHOOL, PATCHAM

THE MAN WHO DIDN'T DIE

A man was walking down a dark road to his friend's house. He then saw a car coming towards him. Suddenly he felt a bullet through his arm. He started walking to his friend's house and his friend took him to the hospital. He came out with an armband.

Zack Gorringe (12)
PATCHAM HIGH SCHOOL, PATCHAM

THE DAY OF A BORED CHILD

A day in the life of a bored child. It was raining.
He was so bored. No one to call, everyone on holiday.
Fidgety, tired, yawning and lots of boring homework.
The electrics went, so no games, computer, TV.
Parents were out. So very bored. Walking around
the house bored.

Sophie Taylor (12)
PATCHAM HIGH SCHOOL, PATCHAM

FUN ON THE FARM

It was a glorious day down on Berrygate Farm.
I wandered down to the chickens. When I arrived at
the gorgeous pen, I was horrified to see the chickens
were pink and headless. They were shaking like leaves
in the wind. I set them free, they rested in a tree.

Lucy Holkham & Jordan Charman (14)
PATCHAM HIGH SCHOOL, PATCHAM

LOVE STORY

Monday, the day I saw him for the thousandth time. The day I realised I was in love! Tuesday, my twelfth birthday, also the best day of my life. The day he asked me out. I couldn't have asked for a better present. Wednesday, we kissed. Thursday, it was over!

Sarah Holman (14)
PATCHAM HIGH SCHOOL, PATCHAM

THE DEAD MUM

A man walked home, his door was open. He went
inside and closed the door. He looked around his
big house, looking for his mum and went in the
living room. She was dead. He called the police.
They came so fast and the man was very sad.

Jack Richardson (14)
PATCHAM HIGH SCHOOL, PATCHAM

133

OH DEAR

I was in my English lesson one day and the teacher told us that he wanted us to write a mini saga. It's this thing where you have to write a story with only fifty words. I didn't understand how anyone could do that in only fifty words.

Toumiee Lokolo (14)
PATCHAM HIGH SCHOOL, PATCHAM

MYTHS AND LEGENDS

There once was a girl called Louise, who didn't believe in myths. One myth was about a mental escapee and a dog. She went to school the next day and had a good day. When she came home, she found her dog dead. The mental man …

Kelsey Johnson (14)
PATCHAM HIGH SCHOOL, PATCHAM

135

THE WALK IN THE WOODS THAT WENT WRONG

One day I was walking through the deep, cold, dark woods, when I kept hearing sticks snapping behind me. I carried on walking through the woods. It was very peaceful. Then I very slowly and very quietly started jogging. I was very scared and jumpy.

Chloe Gill (14)
PATCHAM HIGH SCHOOL, PATCHAM

UNTITLED

Noel Fielding walked into Patcham High School, wearing his ultra-tight, jet-black skinny jeans, followed by Julian Barrat wearing a pink and yellow floral shirt and white cropped trousers. They stood on the main stage in the assembly hall and did a crimpathon with fellow students. They all cheered.

Gabrielle Tilley (13)
PATCHAM HIGH SCHOOL, PATCHAM

DANGER

I was at school, doing my work and I had to stick
things in and the glue had a clue.
It said, 'Everyone will die!'
I went home and on the news something happened
in an avenue. It was an explosion. I should have done
something to help them all!

Sam Dexter (13)
WORTHING HIGH SCHOOL, WORTHING

TORNADO TERROR

Freddy was running for his life, from a twisting tornado.
The rain fell at high speed. It was catching him up and
his heart was racing away, like an F1 car at full speed.
I came, with a hair dryer in one hand and a water gun
in the other.

Ryan Singers (13)
WORTHING HIGH SCHOOL, WORTHING

INFORMATION

We hope you have enjoyed reading this book - and that you will continue to enjoy it in the coming years.

If you like reading and writing, drop us a line or give us a call and we'll send you a free information pack. Alternatively visit our website at www.youngwriters.co.uk

Write to:
Young Writers Information,
Remus House,
Coltsfoot Drive,
Peterborough,
PE2 9JX

Tel: (01733) 890066
Email: youngwriters@forwardpress.co.uk